Words of Love to Color

to Color

Sweet Thoughts to Live and Color by

Eleri Fowler

Sweet Thoughts to Live and Color by

HARPER
An Imprint of HarperCollins*Publishers*

For Mister Leopard

Words of Love to Color: Sweet Thoughts to Live and Color By
By Eleri Fowler
Copyright © 2016 by HarperCollins Publishers

For information address HarperCollins Children's Books,
a division of HarperCollins Publishers, 195 Broadway, New York, NY 10007.
www.harpercollinschildrens.com
ISBN 978-0-06-256608-9

The artist used a pencil, paper, brush pens, fineliner pen, and computer
to create the illustrations for this book.

Typography by Kathleen Duncan
20 21 22 PC/LSCW 10 9 8 7 6 5 4 3
❖
First Edition

This book belongs to

_____

Let love in!

This book is a window into my sketchbook: full of all the wonderful love-inspired scenes and patterns that fill me with warmth. You'll find designs featuring romantic quotes, plus flowers, hearts, lovebirds, and more—all ready for you to make your own!

There are so many creative ways to enjoy this book. The choice is yours—experiment with colored pencils, gel pens, or felt-tip pens. Do try a few test doodles to make sure your pens don't bleed through the paper! If you are using colored pencils, try building up different shades and tones of color within your design. The best way I've found to mix two or more colors together is to layer each color in turn from lightest to darkest. That way, you can control the intensity of the color. If you're feeling a bit daring, try using watercolors! (But be sure to let them dry before turning the page.) Once you've filled your pages with glorious color, why stop there? You can be sure I won't be limited to just coloring—my copy of the book will be bursting with little embellishments like gems, sequins, and glitter. Be creative! I love that no two finished books will look alike: embrace that! The most important thing is to experiment and have fun.

My Influences

Nature has a massive influence on my work. I love to go on long walks in the country and along the coast. My area of Wales is bursting with beautiful gardens and rolling hills, which means inspiration is just outside my front door!

My biggest source of inspiration, however, is travel. It is my absolute passion. I have spent quite a lot of time in Southeast Asia, which is my love, and where I thrive. The abundance of nature, the animals, and breathtaking scenery cannot fail to fill your imagination. I feel so lucky to have a job that lets me work as I travel about, so I always make sure that I have a sketchbook and laptop on hand to start the next project wherever inspiration strikes. Coming home from a trip, I always feel extra energized and full of creativity!

Behind the Scenes—
How I Create My Art to Color

I always start a project with a simple sketch using a mechanical pencil. I am a bit of a perfectionist, so one of my favorite tools in the world is my 0.35mm pencil, as it gives such a smooth, precise line. I like to work on layout paper as it is semitransparent, which is great for tracing. Perhaps I'm a bit old-fashioned, but I like to stick to traditional drawing methods as much as possible and only use the computer for final tweaks for print.

To create my illustrations, first I'll sketch out a rough shape—laying out the main elements in the piece. Then I'll trace over it, adding in more details. I'll repeat this stage a few times until I end up with a piece that I am happy with. Then, I redraw the final image using a black fineliner pen (0.05 is my preference as, just like with my pencil, it gives a very thin and accurate line).

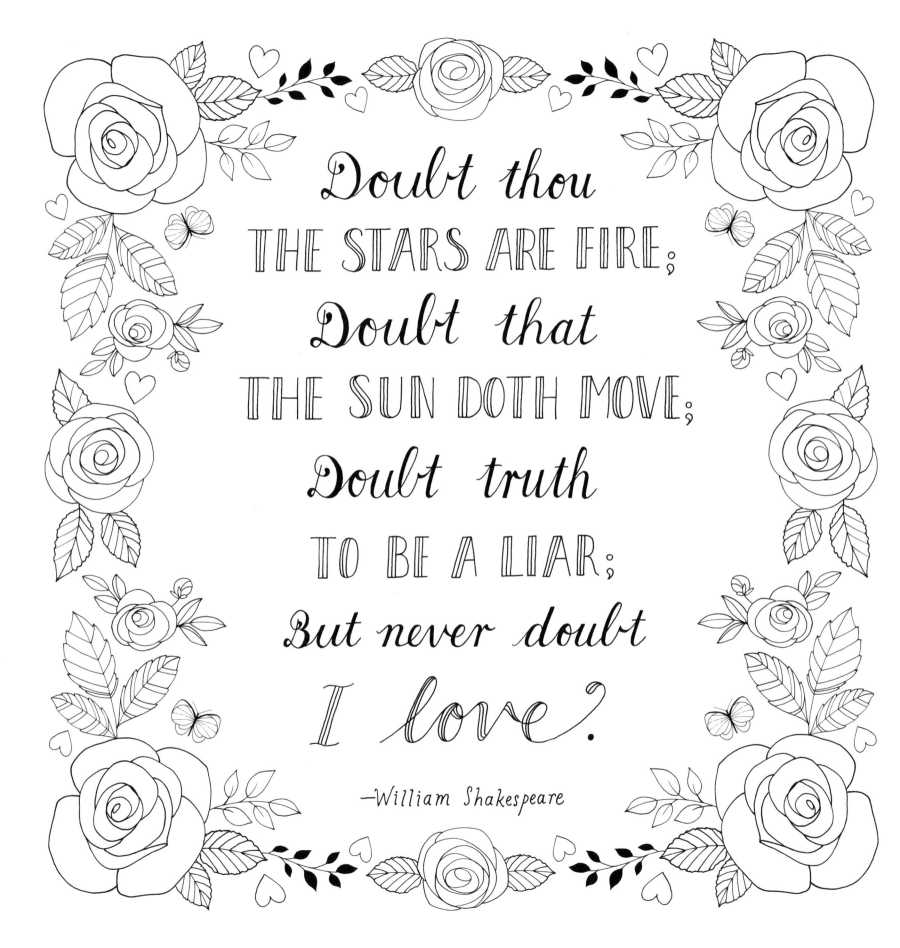

Doubt thou
THE STARS ARE FIRE;
Doubt that
THE SUN DOTH MOVE;
Doubt truth
TO BE A LIAR;
But never doubt
I love.

—William Shakespeare

To get the full value
of a JOY
YOU MUST HAVE SOMEBODY
to divide it with.
—Mark Twain

Each time
YOU HAPPEN TO ME
all over
again.

—Edith Wharton

You must allow me to tell you HOW ARDENTLY I admire and love you.

—Jane Austen

To be
IN LOVE
is to *surpass*
ONE'S SELF.

—Oscar Wilde

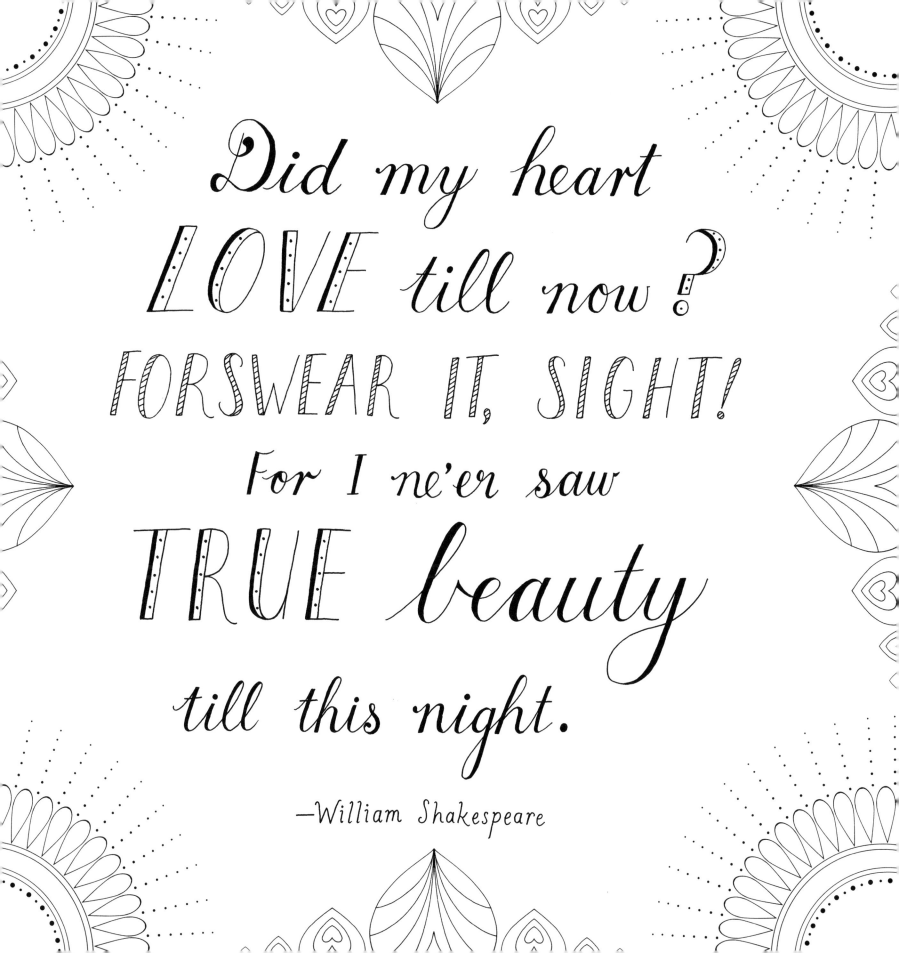

Did my heart LOVE till now? FORSWEAR IT, SIGHT! For I ne'er saw TRUE beauty till this night.

—William Shakespeare

I loved her against REASON, against PROMISE, against PEACE.

—Charles Dickens

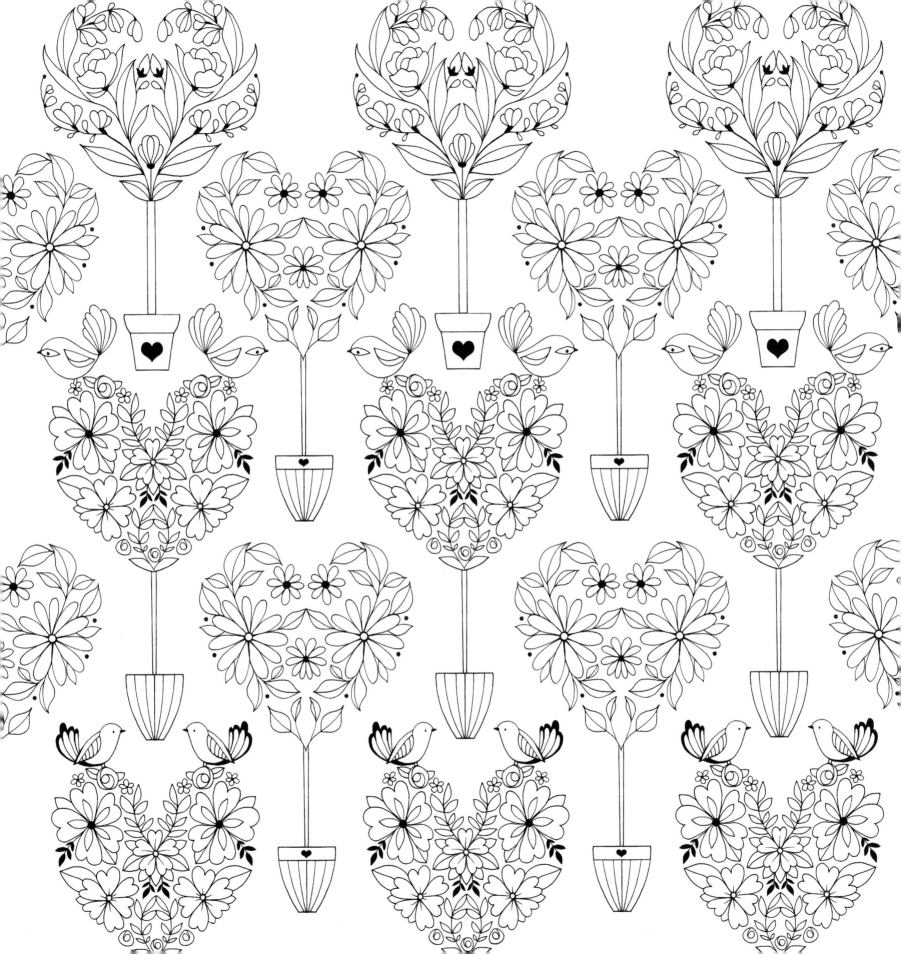

'Tis better to have loved AND LOST THAN NEVER to have lov'd AT ALL.

—Alfred, Lord Tennyson

Love COMFORTETH *like* SUNSHINE *after* rain.

—William Shakespeare

We loved with a love
that was more than love.

—Edgar Allan Poe

How

DO I LOVE THEE?

Let me COUNT the ways.

—Elizabeth Barrett Browning

GOOD NIGHT, good night!
PARTING IS SUCH
sweet sorrow,
THAT I SHALL SAY
good night
till it be MORROW.

—William Shakespeare

Love is not love
WHICH ALTERS
when it
alteration finds.

—William Shakespeare

It has made me better,
LOVING YOU.

—Henry James

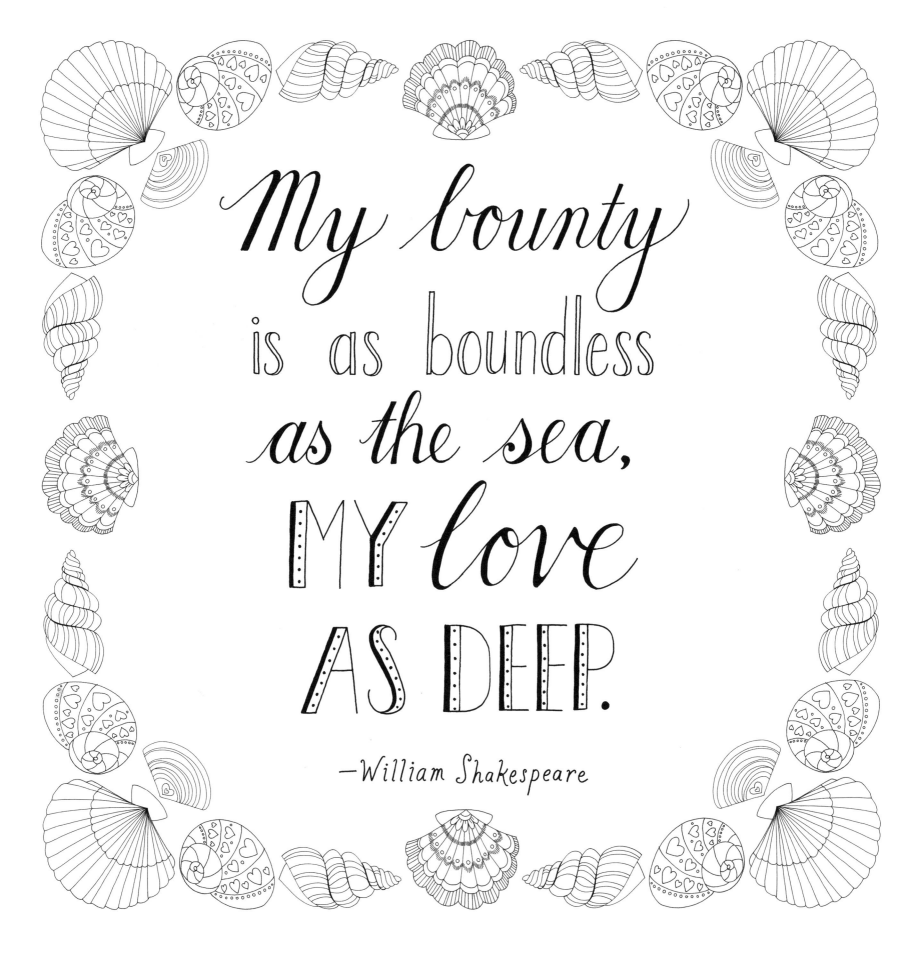

My bounty
is as boundless
as the sea,
MY love
AS DEEP.

—William Shakespeare

There is no other pearl
TO BE FOUND
In the shadowy folds of life.
TO LOVE
is a fulfillment.

—Victor Hugo

He's more myself THAN I AM. Whatever our souls ARE MADE OF, his and mine ARE the SAME.

—Emily Brontë

I wish you TO KNOW that you have been the LAST dream of my soul.

—Charles Dickens

List of Quotes

Doubt thou the stars are fire; Doubt that the sun doth move;
Doubt truth to be a liar; But never doubt I love.
—William Shakespeare

To get the full value of a joy you must have somebody to divide it with.
—Mark Twain

Each time you happen to me all over again.
—Edith Wharton

You must allow me to tell you how ardently I admire and love you.
—Jane Austen

To be in love is to surpass one's self.
—Oscar Wilde

Did my heart love till now? Forswear it, sight!
For I ne'er saw true beauty till this night.
—William Shakespeare

I loved her against reason, against promise, against peace.
—Charles Dickens

Who, being loved, is poor?
—Oscar Wilde

'Tis better to have loved and lost than never to have lov'd at all.
—Alfred, Lord Tennyson

Love comforteth like sunshine after rain.
—William Shakespeare

We loved with a love that was more than love.
—Edgar Allan Poe

How do I love thee? Let me count the ways.
—Elizabeth Barrett Browning

Good night, good night! Parting is such sweet sorrow,
That I shall say good night till it be morrow.
—William Shakespeare

Love is not love
Which alters when it alteration finds.
—William Shakespeare

Life, I tell you, would be impossible without you.
—Virginia Woolf

It has made me better, loving you.
—Henry James

Grow old with me! The best is yet to be.
—Robert Browning

My bounty is as boundless as the sea,
My love as deep.
—William Shakespeare

There is no other pearl to be found in the shadowy folds of life.
To love is a fulfillment.
—Victor Hugo

He's more myself than I am. Whatever our souls are made of,
his and mine are the same.
—Emily Brontë

I wish you to know that you have been the last dream of my soul.
—Charles Dickens

About the Author

I have always loved anything creative, and can't imagine myself doing anything else but art. I studied illustration at university, but since working as a full-time artist, I've found myself experimenting with embroidery and paper cutting, which gives my art depth and texture. After graduating, I started working as an in-house illustrator for a greeting card company, and now I work for myself and have my own collection of cards. I live in the countryside of Wales, and many of the birds and flowers in my art are inspired by long walks along the coast.

I really hope you love coloring this book as much as I loved drawing it!

Eleri